Dear Parents:

Congratulations! Your child is taking the first steps on an exciting journey. The destination? Independent reading!

STEP INTO READING® will help your child get there. The program offers five steps to reading success. Each step includes fun stories and colorful art or photographs. In addition to original fiction and books with favorite characters, there are Step into Reading Non-Fiction Readers, Phonics Readers and Boxed Sets, Sticker Readers, and Comic Readers—a complete literacy program with something to interest every child.

Learning to Read, Step by Step!

Ready to Read   Preschool–Kindergarten
• big type and easy words • rhyme and rhythm • picture clues
For children who know the alphabet and are eager to begin reading.

Reading with Help   Preschool–Grade 1
• basic vocabulary • short sentences • simple stories
For children who recognize familiar words and sound out new words with help.

Reading on Your Own   Grades 1–3
• engaging characters • easy-to-follow plots • popular topics
For children who are ready to read on their own.

Reading Paragraphs   Grades 2–3
• challenging vocabulary • short paragraphs • exciting stories
For newly independent readers who read simple sentences with confidence.

Ready for Chapters   Grades 2–4
• chapters • longer paragraphs • full-color art
For children who want to take the plunge into chapter books but still like colorful pictures.

STEP INTO READING® is designed to give every child a successful reading experience. The grade levels are only guides; children will progress through the steps at their own speed, developing confidence in their reading. The F&P Text Level on the back cover serves as another tool to help you choose the right book for your child.

Remember, a lifetime love of reading starts with a single step!

PHOEBE DUNN was a world-renowned photographer known especially for her pictures of children and animals. Her timeless images, photographed in natural settings, using natural light, uniquely capture the interactions and relationships between children and their pets. Phoebe photographed the world as she knew it, capturing the feelings and relationships that make us all human. Her photographs have been published around the world in more than twenty children's books, a number of them written by her daughter, Judy Dunn.

Text copyright © 1976, renewed 2004 by Judy Dunn Spangenberg
Abridged text copyright © 2017 by Judy Dunn Spangenberg
Cover and interior photographs copyright © 1976 by Phoebe Dunn,
renewed 2004 by Judy Dunn Spangenberg and Tristram Dunn
New photographs copyright © 2017 by The Phoebe Dunn Collection

Step into Reading, Random House, and the Random House colophon are registered trademarks of Penguin Random House LLC.

Visit us on the Web!
StepIntoReading.com
randomhousekids.com

Educators and librarians, for a variety of teaching tools, visit us at
RHTeachersLibrarians.com

Library of Congress Cataloging-in-Publication Data
Dunn, Judy.
The little duck / story by Judy Dunn ; photographs by Phoebe Dunn. — Abridged edition.
pages cm. — (Step into reading. Level 1)
"This is an abridged edition of The Little Duck, originally published in a different form in the United States by Random House Children's Books, New York, in 1976."
Summary: Henry the duck grows up and sets out to see the world around him, making special friends along the way.
ISBN 978-0-553-53352-1 (pb) — ISBN 978-0-553-53353-8 (glb)
[1. Ducks—Fiction. 2. Domestic animals—Fiction.] I. Dunn, Phoebe, illustrator. II. Title.
PZ7.D92158 Ld 2016 [E]—dc23 2014040442

Printed in the United States of America
10 9 8 7 6 5 4 3 2 1

This book has been officially leveled by using the F&P Text Level Gradient™ Leveling System.

The Little Duck

by Judy Dunn

photographs by Phoebe Dunn

Random House 🏠 New York

One day
a little boy
was fishing.

He saw an egg
in the grass.
He took it home.

He kept the egg warm.

One day

the shell cracked open.

The little duck
had hatched.
The boy named him
Henry.

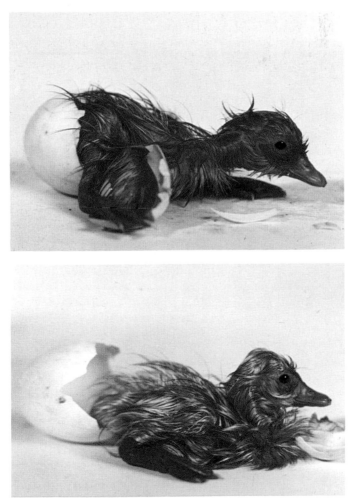

His feathers were wet.

His feet were
so big!

Henry stretched

his wings.

His feathers began
to dry.
He was
almost fluffy.

Henry was tired
from hatching.

He took a

little nap.

The little boy
let Henry swim
in a little pool.

He helped Henry
dry off.

Henry made friends

with the boy's dog.

He ate a lot of food.

Henry grew bigger
and bigger.

His white feathers
were growing in.

He followed the little boy
around the farm.

Henry talked to
the hen.

He talked to

the white rabbit.

And he met a kid.

A kid is a baby goat.

Henry and the boy
were happy.

Henry still tried
to swim in
his little pool.

But it was too small.

Henry wanted a bigger place to swim.

One day
he went
for a walk.

He was happy to find
a big pond.

He saw a girl duck
swimming.

Henry went
to say hello.

The other duck's name
was Emma.

The two ducks went
swimming together.

One day
Henry and Emma
had an egg
of their own!